Little Whale

Jo Weaver

PEACHTREE
ATLANTA

Gray Whale led her baby out of the shallows
and into the warm southern sea.

"Where are we going?" asked Little Whale.

"Follow me," said Gray Whale.

The rest of their family had already left to find food in the cool, rich waters of the North. It was time to join them.

"We're going on a long journey, Little Whale,"
sang Gray Whale. "We're going home."

A great forest beneath
them drifted with the tide.

"What's home?" wondered Little Whale.
"Maybe this is it?"

But Gray Whale kept on swimming.

The coral reef sparkled
with life. Strange new
creatures swam all
around them.

"Is this home?"
asked Little Whale.

"No, we've still got a long way to go,"
said Gray Whale, nudging her
Little Whale onwards.

Together, they traveled mile after mile
under vast midnight skies.

"Are we nearly there?" asked Little Whale.

"Not yet," sang Gray Whale,
and northwards they swam,
through seas that
shimmered and danced.

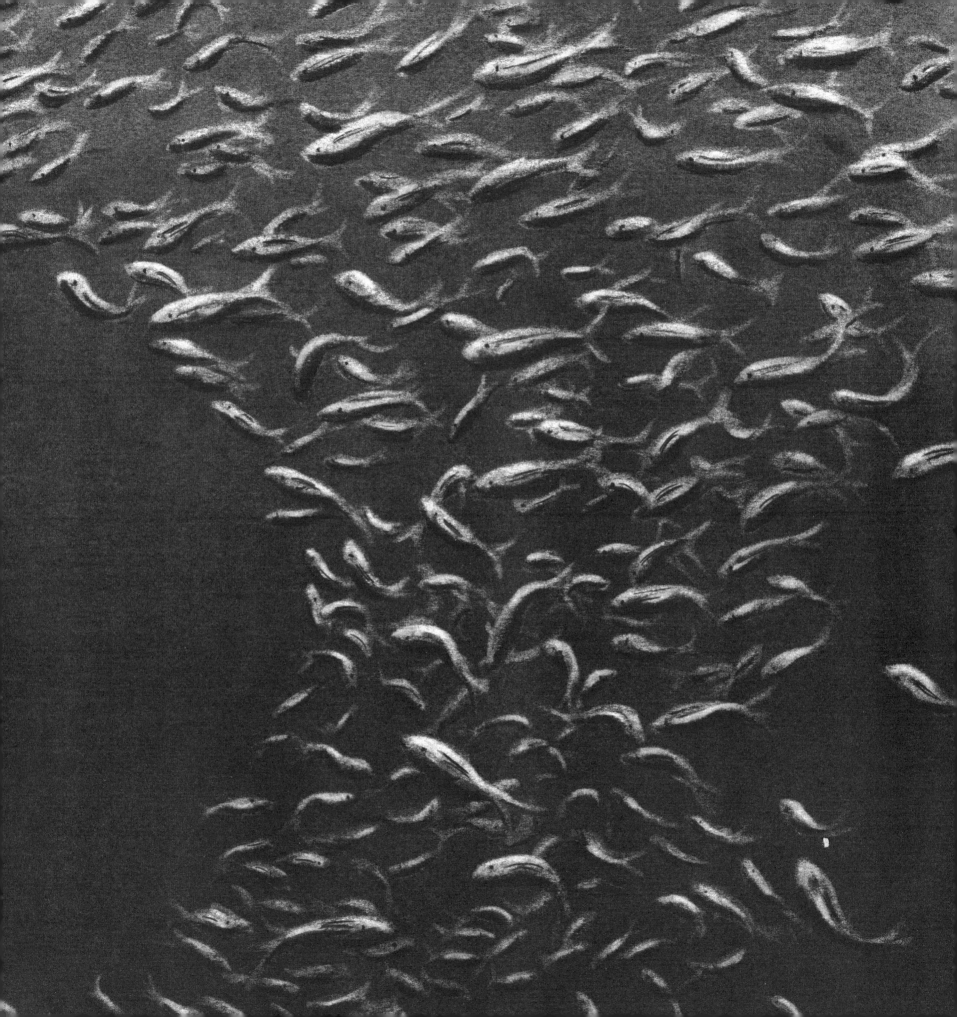

Days and nights passed.
The water grew colder and deeper and darker.

"Are we nearly home yet?" Little Whale asked.

But Little Whale's voice was lost
in the noise of passing ships.

Little Whale felt very small.
There was no one in sight except Gray Whale.

Suddenly they were no longer alone. Orcas were trailing them, and Little Whale knew they were very dangerous.

"I'm scared," said Little Whale.

"I'm right beside you, keep going!" urged Gray Whale.

But Little Whale's strength was fading.

"Hold on to me!"
said Gray Whale.

Little Whale clung on to Gray Whale,
and they surged through the water,
leaving the danger far behind.

"I'm so tired!" murmured Little Whale.
"Will we ever get there?"

At long last, the sound of whale song
echoed through the icy water.

"Who is that?" asked Little Whale.

"It's our family," said Gray Whale.
"They're calling us home."

Sunshine glittered on the mountain peaks,
as the pod of gray whales sang their welcome.

"We made it! We're home in the North!" said Gray Whale,
and she nuzzled her brave Little Whale.

"So this is it!" said Little Whale. "We're home."

Resting safely against the warmth of Gray Whale,
with family all around, Little Whale drifted off to sleep.

Gray whales migrate up to 12,400 miles every year—a journey that is believed to be the longest annual migration of any mammal. The whales swim south to breed in the late autumn and return to their northern feeding grounds in the spring. Young calves make this epic journey alone with their mother.

For my little artists: Eliza, Geordie, Jemima, Annie, Raffy, and Rowan, of course. X

Ω

Published by
PEACHTREE PUBLISHERS
1700 Chattahoochee Avenue
Atlanta, Georgia 30318-2112
www.peachtree-online.com

Text and illustrations © 2018 by Jo Weaver

First published in Great Britain in 2018 by Hodder Children's Books,
an imprint of Hachette Children's Group
First United States version published in 2018 by Peachtree Publishers
First United States trade paperback edition published in 2018 by Peachtree Publishers

The illustrations were rendered in charcoal.

Printed in China
10 9 8 7 6 5 4 3 2 1 (hardcover)
10 9 8 7 6 5 4 3 2 1 (trade paperback)
First Edition

HC: 978-1-68263-049-5
PB: 978-1-68263-074-7

Library of Congress Cataloging-in-Publication Data

Names: Weaver, Jo (Children's author), author, illustrator.
Title: Little Whale / Jo Weaver.
Description: Atlanta : Peachtree Publishers, 2018. | "First published in Great Britain in 2018 by Hodder Children's Books." | Summary: Little Whale is nervous about leaving the shallows of the warm, southern sea, but Gray Whale gently guides her new baby as they migrate to the cool, rich waters of the north. Identifiers: LCCN 2017041172 | ISBN 9781682630495
Subjects: LCSH: Gray whale—Juvenile fiction. | CYAC: Gray whale—Fiction. | Whales—Fiction. Mammals—Migration—Fiction. | Parental behavior in animals—Fiction. Classification: LCC PZ10.3.W353 Ll 2018 | DDC [E]—dc23 LC record available at https://lccn.loc.gov/2017041172